A Time
For Remembering

BY **Chuck Thurman**

PICTURES BY **Elizabeth Sayles**

Simon and Schuster
Books for Young Readers
PUBLISHED BY SIMON & SCHUSTER INC., NEW YORK

Simon and Schuster Books for Young Readers
Simon & Schuster Building, Rockefeller Center
1230 Avenue of the Americas, New York, New York 10020

Simon and Schuster Books for Young Readers
is a trademark of Simon & Schuster Inc.
Manufactured in the United States of America

10 9 8 7 6 5 4 3 2 1

Library of Congress Cataloging-in-Publication Data
Thurman, Chuck.   A time for remembering/by Chuck Thurman;
illustrated by Elizabeth Sayles.   p.   cm.
Summary: After his grandfather's death, a boy remembers the intimate
experience they shared and follows his grandfather's last request.
[1. Grandfathers—Fiction.   2. Death—Fiction.]   I. Sayles,
Elizabeth, ill.   II. Title.   89-5969
PZ7.T42235Ti   1989   CIP
[E]—dc19   AC
ISBN 0-671-68573-2

To my grandfathers, and to my sons
—C.T.

To my father, and to Anthony
—E.S.

The boy sat by the fireplace in his grandfather's house, holding the faded yellow flower. The grown-ups had been unusually serious, and some of them had cried. Now it was good to be alone, and to hear their voices murmuring in the other room. The voices made him feel warm in a different way from the fire.

Most of the day, the boy had felt in the way,
but now he had something important to do.
He stared into the fire and watched it dance
around the logs his grandfather had cut.

He remembered the time his grandfather showed him how logs were split with a sledge hammer and a wedge. He remembered how his grandfather smelled, and how he wiped his forehead with his handkerchief. He remembered a squirrel that ran away when they got to the woodpile.

He remembered the time he broke his grandmother's vase and how his mother got so mad. He remembered his grandfather had taken him outside and asked him if he understood what he had done wrong. When the boy said yes, his grandfather had taken him to the store and bought them both candy.

He remembered the time his grandfather sold him a pocket knife. His grandfather said it was bad luck just to give somebody a knife, so he had sold it to the boy for a penny.

He remembered his grandfather's laugh, and the funny glasses he wore. He remembered a photograph of his grandfather surrounded by a lot of dogs. He remembered his grandfather's old car.

He remembered the last time he saw his
grandfather. It was in the white hospital where
everything smelled so strange. His whole family
was there, but his grandfather asked them all
to step outside the room so he could have
some time alone with the boy.

They talked about school, and about the hospital. While they talked, his grandfather picked some wilted flowers from a plant near his bed. He told the boy it would make the plant stronger so it could produce more flowers. Then his grandfather asked the boy to do an important thing.

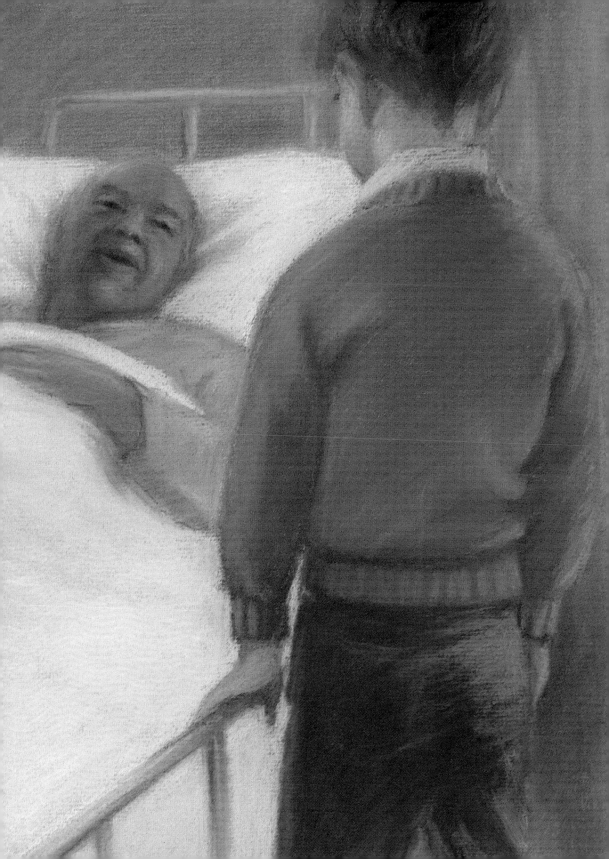

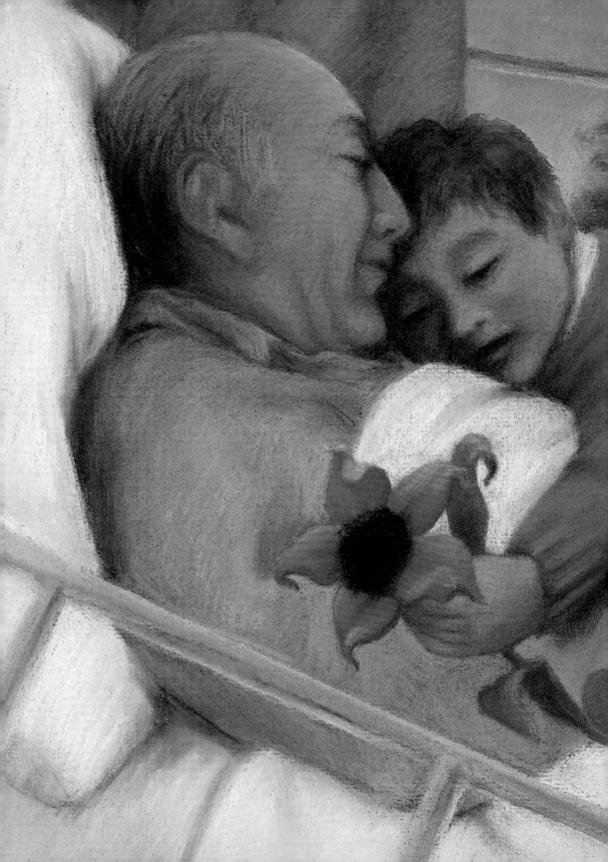

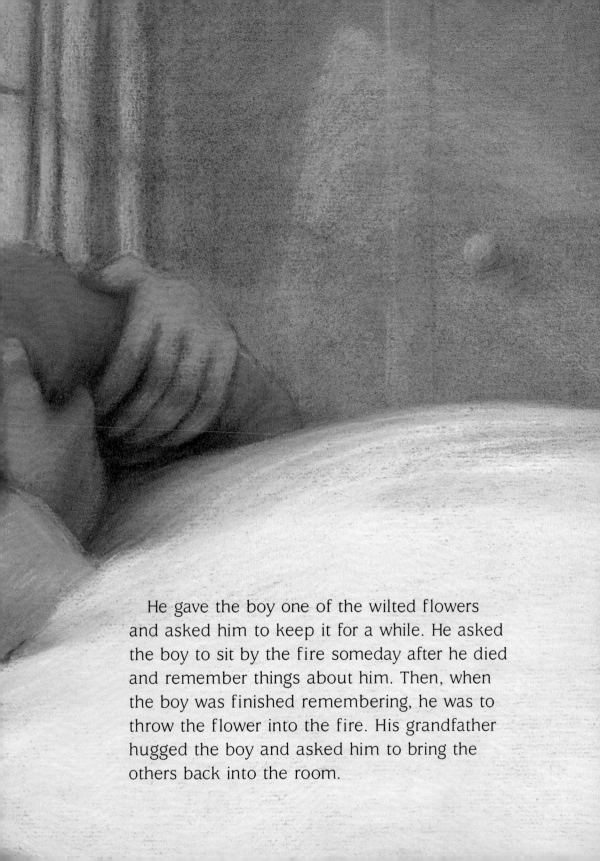

He gave the boy one of the wilted flowers
and asked him to keep it for a while. He asked
the boy to sit by the fire someday after he died
and remember things about him. Then, when
the boy was finished remembering, he was to
throw the flower into the fire. His grandfather
hugged the boy and asked him to bring the
others back into the room.

The boy looked at the now dry flower and
remembered that last hug. He threw the flower
into the fire and watched it become part of the
flames. Then the boy cried a little and, after a
while, went to be with the grown-ups.

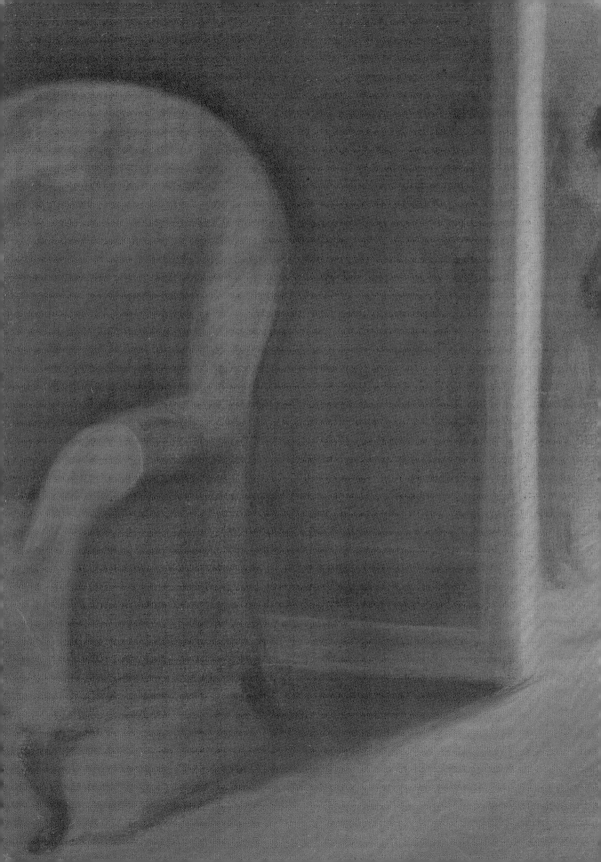